Iris and Walter
The Sleepover

Iris and Walter
The Sleepover

WRITTEN BY

Elissa Haden Guest

ILLUSTRATED BY

Christine Davenier

GULLIVER BOOKS
HARCOURT, INC.
SAN DIEGO   NEW YORK   LONDON

For Nathanael, with all my love—E. H. G.

For my dear friend John Martini—C. D.

Text copyright © 2002 by Elissa Haden Guest
Illustrations copyright © 2002 by Christine Davenier

www.HarcourtBooks.com

Gulliver Books is a trademark of Harcourt, Inc., registered
in the United States of America and/or other jurisdictions.

Library of Congress Cataloging-in-Publication Data
Guest, Elissa Haden.
Iris and Walter, the sleepover/written by Elissa Haden Guest;
illustrated by Christine Davenier.
p. cm.
"Gulliver Books."
Summary: Iris's first sleepover at her friend Walter's house
ends early when Iris gets homesick and wants to go home.
[1. Sleepovers—Fiction. 2. Homesickness—Fiction.]
I. Davenier, Christine, ill. II. Title.
PZ7.G9375Iv 2002
[E]—dc21   2001005259
ISBN 0-15-216487-1

First edition
H G F E D C B A
MANUFACTURED IN CHINA

Contents

1. Big Plans

Iris couldn't wait for Saturday.
On Saturday, Iris was going
to sleep over at her best friend
Walter's house.
It was all she could talk about.

"It will be my *first* sleepover, Grandpa," said Iris. "How exciting!" said Grandpa.

"Walter and I are going to put on a puppet show," Iris told her mother. "What fun!" said Iris's mother.

"And we're going to ride Rain
in our pajamas," Iris told her father.
"You don't say," said Iris's father.

9

"And we're going to sleep out on Walter's porch and stay up very, very late," Iris told Baby Rose. "That's what big kids do on sleepovers, Rosie."

"Okay, my big girl, hop into bed,"
said Iris's mother.
Iris's mother read a story.

Grandpa sang the girls a song.

Iris's father
tucked them in.

"Good night, little Rosie," he said.
"Good night, my Iris," he said.
Then Iris's mother turned on
the night-light and closed the door.

2. Worries

The next day at school, Iris told
her friends about the sleepover.
"Sleepovers are fun," said Armando.
"You can stay up all night," said Lulu.
"And have pillow fights," said Jenny.
"Wow!" said Iris and Walter.
Benny didn't say a word.

But after lunch, Benny whispered,
"I don't like sleepovers."
"You don't?" asked Iris.

"No. I like to sleep in my own room,
in my own bed," said Benny.
"One time, I went to sleep over
at my cousin's house, but…"
"But what?" asked Iris.

"I got really homesick," said Benny.
"Why?" asked Iris.
"Because," said Benny, "I missed
my pillow."
"What did you do?" asked Iris.
"My aunt had to take me home
in the middle of the night," he answered.
"Oh," said Iris.

I hope that doesn't happen to me,
she thought.

3. The Sleepover

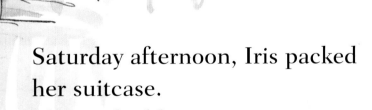

Saturday afternoon, Iris packed
her suitcase.
She packed her cozy pajamas.
She packed her favorite doll, Pearl.
And she packed her baby pillow,
so she wouldn't get homesick.
Baby Rose watched from her crib.

"Now, Rosie," said Iris, "I'm not going
to be here tonight because
I'm sleeping over at Walter's.
Remember?"
Baby Rose gave Iris a big smile.

"But Mama will still read a story,
and Grandpa will sing a song,
and Daddy will tuck you in.
And when you're a big girl,
you'll go on a sleepover, too."
Baby Rose said, "Ba, ba, ba."

"Okay, I'm ready to go to Walter's,"
said Iris.
"Have fun, my Iris," said Iris's mother.
"We'll see you tomorrow,"
said Iris's father.
"So long, everybody!" said Iris.

Grandpa and Iris drove over to Walter's.

"Come in, Iris," said Walter's father. "Would you like some cookies?" asked Walter's mother. "Let's go play!" said Walter.

Iris and Walter put on a puppet show.

They rode Rain in their pajamas.

They sat on
the porch
and watched
the stars
come out.

"I think sleepovers are great," said Iris.
"I'm not homesick at all."
"We should have a sleepover
every week!" said Walter.
Iris and Walter drank hot cocoa
and shared the last cookie.

Then Walter's mother said,
"It's getting late, kids. Time for bed."
Iris thought about home.
She wondered if Baby Rose was still
awake and if Rosie missed her.

Walter's mother kissed Walter good night.
Then she kissed Iris.
"Good night, sleep tight," said Walter's father.
"I'm not sleepy, are you?" asked Iris.
"No," said Walter, yawning.
"Let's stay up *all* night," said Iris.

"What do you want to do?" asked Walter.
"Let's tell stories," said Iris.
"Okay," said Walter, "you go first.
I'll just get comfortable."
Walter snuggled down into his sleeping bag.
He was warm and cozy.

Iris told Walter a long, long, *long* story.
When she was finished, she said,
"Now it's your turn, Walter. *Walter?*"
But there was no sound.

"Walter," whispered Iris,
"it's your turn to tell a story."
But Walter was fast asleep.

4. Home Sweet Home

It was very quiet on the porch.
Iris hugged Pearl close.
She tried to get comfortable.
Suddenly, Iris felt all alone.
She missed her mother's stories.
She missed Grandpa's songs.

She missed the way
her father tucked her in
and kissed her good night.
And she missed sleeping
in her own room,
in her own bed, with her
own baby sister close by.

"Walter," Iris whispered in the dark.
"*Walter*, wake up."
Iris gave Walter a little shake.
"Huh?" said Walter.
"Walter," said Iris,
"I think I want to go home."

"You do?" Walter asked. "Why?"
"I'm homesick," said Iris,
and she started to cry.
"Gosh," said Walter.
He went to get his mother.

"Iris, honey, are you sure
you want to go home?"
asked Walter's mother.
"Yes, I'm sure," said Iris.
"It's okay—we'll take you home,"
said Walter's mother.
"You can sleep over another time.
Right, Walter?"
"Sure," said Walter.

Iris packed her suitcase,
and climbed into the car.
"We're going home now, Pearl,"
she whispered.
The drive seemed to take forever.

40

But when she arrived, *everyone* was waiting.
"Welcome home," said Iris's father.
"How about a hug?" asked Iris's mother.
"Why, Iris, you've grown," said Grandpa.
Iris laughed, and hugged them all.

Then she went into her own room
and climbed into her own bed.
Her own Baby Rose was fast asleep close by.
Iris's mother kissed Iris good night.
"I'll sleep over at Walter's another time,"
said Iris, yawning.

"Of course you will," said her mother.
  And she did.

The illustrations in this book were created in pen-and-ink on keacolor paper.
The display type was set in Elroy.
The text type was set in Fairfield Medium.
Color separations by Bright Arts Ltd., Hong Kong
Manufactured by South China Printing Company, Ltd., China
This book was printed on totally chlorine-free Nymolla Matte Art paper.
Production supervision by Sandra Grebenar and Pascha Gerlinger
Designed by Lydia D'moch